THAT, WHICH CLOUDS THE SOUL

By Nicolas Ryan Moore

An Idea Machine Output Publication

Published in 2017 by Idea Machine Output

Idea Machine Output books may be purchased for educational, business, or sales promotional use. For information, please email info@ideamachineoutput.com

This is a work of fiction. Any resemblance to actual persons, living or dead, events, or locales is entirely coincidental.

Cover Designed by Leah Odom

ISBN-13: 978-0-692-86910-9

To:

Hannah & Ozlo

For the past

The Pious Commonwealth rules
within the walls of The City.

All is well for those who abide
by their rules and laws.

Those who don't, have much to fear.

Not only will they have to answer to
The Pious Commonwealth,
but they will have to answer to
The Holy Being, above them.

That fear keeps them in line.

That fear runs The City.

I.

The White Amongst The Blue, which brushed across His face, was softer than any linen He'd ever known. He pushed through it and found that it was coarse within its rounded edges. It had a well-worn roughness to it, as though it had brushed against many faces before Him. For some reason that feeling gave Him comfort and He paused briefly in the middle of it all to bask in the state of, what He didn't know was, happiness.

Something was calling to Him, though, so He shouldn't stay long. He knew not what it was, but He knew He must leave the comfort of The White Amongst The Blue and continue on the quest that was welling inside of Him and so He drifted through it, reemerging on the other side. Then, He found Himself in the middle of The Vast Blue.

A rush of air caught itself in His tunic and propelled Him further onward through The Blue. He was flying without wings, unlike The Angels, which He knew so well. The speed in which He traveled increased as He moved on. He passed more clusters of Whites Amongst The Blue, breaking through a few; yet He was now moving too quickly to feel the comfort He'd felt before.

Then, all of a sudden, He stopped and there was unimaginable beauty before Him. It was orange and yellow and the light it emitted warmed His skin and that warmth radiated through Him. The calm He'd felt in The White Amongst The Blue paled in comparison to the feeling that was emanating from the yellow-orange orb inches away from His face. The warmth grew in Him like a tree; it's branches reached out through His arms and fingers. A great calm resonated within Him. He shut His eyes. He basked in the glory.

It's then that the trumpets sounded.

His alarm reverberated off the white, stone walls of the compartment, and it caused The Man to wake. Immediately, He wished He had not awoken. He wished it even after He'd walked into the little washroom provided to Him. Even after He stood, staring at His reflection in the immaculate mirror above the sink. He found His eye sockets darker than the rest of His face (a subtle sign that peaceful sleep evaded Him most nights). Within those sockets, His eyes sat, bloodshot and weary.

He let out a sigh, the manner of which His mouth, throat, and lungs were all accustomed to exhaling. He rubbed His cheeks with the palms of His hands. The hair on His face had grown out. It was a shaggy sort of stubble. It was patchy, granted, but long enough for Him to have taken a liking to it, despite what The Director of Nourishment, His Superior, had to say on the matter. He didn't want to shave it, but He knew He must.

Unfortunately, in The City, there were certain rules every man, woman, and child were expected to adhere to. One of which was to be clean-shaven on certain days throughout one's life. Today was one of those days. So, with chagrin, The Man lathered His face and began to shave off a little bit of Himself.

The Woman was awake before Her alarm sounded. She lay there in Her bed, looking at The Cross hanging on the ceiling above Her. She knew She would be lying if She had said She wasn't excited, but there would also be untruth in a statement denying

Her nervousness. She just did not know if She was more one or the other. Her stomach had grown sick from the knots and butterflies trading places over and over again.

When Her stomach became too much for Her to handle, She saw Herself to the washroom and wretched up most of the nerves. After She'd washed Her face and mouth, She looked at Herself in the mirror and began to examine what it reflected back to Her. She then found Herself wondering if She could do what was being asked of Her.

From school She had learned, before The Pious Commonwealth had taken over and banished The Heathens, that what She was about to undertake had been much more difficult. Goods and services were once traded for paper that was used to acquire lavish decorations and accoutrements for the task She and another were about to undertake. She even heard about a horror called 'The Wedding Night', which was only hinted at in a book She had once read in The Library, before The Pious Commonwealth decided that books were not a necessity The Citizens should be privy to. She had asked Her Matron about it and received horrifying details She did not like to think about. She was told not to worry about it though; Pairings were now simple affairs. Yet still, She wondered about it all. Would She be a good Partner? Was She cut from the cloth of Rearers? Or perhaps, most importantly, would He like Her?

There had never been an unsuccessful Pairing before (at least none that She'd ever heard of) and the thought that She may be responsible for the first frightened Her. All She had ever wanted to be was a good Partner and Rearer.

The Man found Himself wondering if She would be pretty. He knew, truly, it did not matter; the choice in Partner was not His to make. Also, Her appearance should not matter to Him, for The Impotence bestowed on Him at Birth made the consideration moot. He had discovered, though, that with a great deal of thought and time, He could conquer it. That's why He thought it. That's why He wondered what She would look like. Although Her looks meant absolutely nothing, for He could not tell Her of His ability. If She told anyone, the prosecution would be swift and fierce. He didn't know exactly what would happen, and perhaps that made Him fear it all the more. Furthermore, even if She didn't tattle, all women in The City were instilled with a great deal of fear towards Lust. He didn't want His new partner to fear Him. That would make for a long and stressful Pairing.

Yet, so would it be if She were beautiful. If Her tunic clung to Her in a certain way, would He be able to hold back His thoughts? He looked down at Himself in His undergarments, and knew He probably couldn't. Just the thought of what She could be was enough to give Him away.

He pondered about relieving Himself now, but He didn't like to do that before He was to see anyone. He felt the guilt would be strewn upon His face and He'd be found out the moment anyone laid eyes on Him. So instead He showered, flogged, and then showered again, after which, He put on His tan tunic.

He liked the way that particular tunic looked on His skin. He thought it complemented the color of His hair. He knew it was foolish to care about His appearance (if not slightly Vain), but He couldn't help it. He wanted to look handsome, just incase She was pretty.

The Woman combed Her hair for far longer than She

should have. If The Matron had come in and seen Her, She surely would have been given a flogging for Vanity right then and there. However, The Woman knew that She would be given privacy today, so that She could prepare appropriately and get used to doing things on Her own. She was also meant to Pray, but She drew a bath instead.

As She soaked, She wondered. Who would The Man She was Partnering with be? Would He be naïve and innocent like Adam? Or strong and wise like Solomon? Perhaps He could be valiant and brave like Moses? He could even be pure and perfect, like Christ himself, but She doubted that very much. Not because She believed what She was told about Christ and how his perfection would go unmatched, but because She had Her own notion about Christ's portrayal in The Book. It was a notion She dare not utter aloud for fear of flogging.

The thought of The Cleansing Rope made Her touch the scars upon Her back. The feel of them made Her mood shift and She no longer felt like bathing. She began to drain the washbasin and towel off. As She dried Herself, She picked out what She would wear.

While She debated which tunic to dawn, She realized

Her future Partner could be pathetic, like Job. That thought frightened Her dearly.

The Man waited silently in the greeting room of His compartment. It was to be the last time He would ever be there. Yet, that is not why He was tapping His foot anxiously.

He was staring at The Cross that hung on the wall. Many thoughts entered His mind as He gazed upon it. All of them brought Him shame. He quickly decided to think of something else. He shifted His gaze.

It didn't matter where He looked, however, for the guilt had already taken a hold of Him. He felt nervous about missing work. He hadn't missed a single day since He was drafted into His job at age fifteen. It had taken everything in Him to present Himself at work every day since then. Now that the streak had ended, He worried that He might make a habit out of it. For a long while now He had a sense of worthlessness growing larger and larger inside Him as He worked each day. That day was the first day that He had felt as though maybe there was something important inside of Him since He'd started working all those years ago.

He had shaved for the first time when He started employment for The Director of Nourishment, shortly after Drafting Day. He had cut His upper lip quite badly. It was awful and embarrassing. Perhaps that is why He did not enjoy shaving. Today was different, though. He had shaved almost perfectly. He took solace in that fact. He looked decent and He surely would be found Pair-worthy by His new Partner. At least He hoped He would.

Images of what She could be began to conjure themselves in His head again as He stared down at the white, stainless carpet at His feet. His mind led itself to other thoughts and He let it wander there. He brought His hand beneath His tunic, absentmindedly, and touched Himself. He closed His hand around it tightly, gripping it with gentle force.

He then stopped suddenly. He realized He shouldn't do it. Not on the special day before Him. If He were captured and taken to The Complex of Judas on Pairing Day that would be a pockmark on not just Him, but The Pious Commonwealth as a whole. He didn't want that day to be sullied by His impure thoughts. He contemplated another flogging, but that's when a knock came from the door. He took a moment to push the thoughts away and then He went to answer it.

There, in the corridor outside His compartment, stood four Guardians and His Escort. The Escort entered the compartment abruptly and with haste, a trait The Man remembered from when He first met His Escort on Drafting Day. The Escort then handed an ornate badge to The Man, which would allow Him safe passage through the corridors of The City during that time of day. The Man didn't much like the color of the badge, but He took it anyway and pinned it to His tunic. He didn't want to be confused for a man missing work. That would be Sloth. The Man knew that if He were to be confused with a Slothful person, He would spend some unwanted time in The Complex of Judas. Even a wild accusation could earn anyone a lifetime in there.

The Escort then cleared his throat and motioned for The Man to exit His compartment for the last time. He looked around the shabby space one more time before He walked out the door. The Man was ready to be done with the compartment and with His Escort as well, for that matter.

The Escort and Guardians then led The Man down the corridors in the direction of The Main Church.

As He eyed all the corridors and sub-corridors along the way, He noted how similar they all were. They were all identically white-on-white and for that He was glad He had The Escort; He frequently would find Himself lost, especially when He was going somewhere He did not frequent very often (He only visited The Main Church on special occasions such as Christ's Mass and Resurrection Day Service, and even then He traveled with a large group of people).

As they drew closer to their destination, The Man could not help but let out a sigh. It was a long, drawn-out exhale, one that was rich with anxiety, a tinge of boredom on its tail. He couldn't control it. It just escaped His mouth as He tilted His head up to look at the plain white ceiling above Him.

The Escort cleared his throat (a nasty habit of his) and The Guardians snorted, whether from disgust or amusement, The Man couldn't tell. Either way, He felt a shiver of shame creep up His spine. He quickly coughed, awkwardly, and stared forward, counting the steps down the hall, wishing with all His might that He could erase that moment in time.

He hated feeling embarrassed. It was a feeling His mind forced Him to wallow in. He knew that later

He would think of that moment. He would shake His head and hate Himself as He hated Himself now. All He could do, though, was continue to walk down the corridor that led from The Complex of John and into The Main Church.

As they entered The Main Church, The Man had expected more pomp. Instead, He was merely received by The Sermon Sayer who led Him to His own Rearers and (He could only assume) The Rearers of The Woman He was to be Paired with, so that He could say hello. After the formalities, He was then led up to The Altar where He stood and waited for Her.

The Woman had chosen to wear Her white tunic (it was, She thought She knew, a custom of old). After She dressed, She then called in The Matron for approval. When She saw Her Matron enter, She almost wept. She had truly grown to adore Her Matron, and even though they hadn't seen eye-to-eye very often, The Matron was a better teacher and caregiver than The Woman's own Rearers had been. It was for that reason (and no others) that She had requested one last Prayer with The Matron.

They both knelt on the floor by The Woman's bed, holding hands, and closing their eyes. The Matron led grace. As she droned on and on, The Woman's mind began to drift off, somewhere else.

As She often did, She wondered about times of old, back when The Heathens ruled the world. How different was the ritual She was about to undertake from those times? She'd heard things from here and there and had been able to piece things together for Herself. The information was mainly gathered from ancient texts and the books in school that weren't really made to teach anything. She found out a lot through inference. The Church let little slip through about what The Heathens were like. She found if She dug deep, though, She could actually figure things out about them on Her own.

She had come to know that if She'd been alive in those older times that the current day would be called Her 'Wedding Day' and She would have been able to choose Her own 'Husband'. Despite how whimsical that all sounded, though, there were good things about not being a Heathen as well. She thought again about 'The Wedding Night'.

After they were 'Wed', 'The Husband' and 'The Wife'

(as She would have been called) would be put into a room together and they would 'Consummate' their 'Marriage'. The Woman had been told that the 'Consummation Ritual' consisted of "The Husband' taking something-or-other from between his legs and placing it inside of "The Wife' where water was made. That was all apparently done in a very painful manner. When The Matron had told The Woman of 'Marriage,' She was stricken with nightmares for weeks. She couldn't stop thinking of all the blood that would come from there. Blood from where water was made sounded awful and unimaginable.

She didn't like thinking about that, even the concept of 'Consummation' was unfathomable. Every woman had been told of the horrors that could come from it. In addition to that, She knew She was something called Barren (whatever that meant) and that something called The Impotence was injected into all males before their Submission on The Day of Family. That apparently stopped a man's need to hurt women in that old manner. She viewed it all as a small price to pay for a painless Pairing. Why would such a thing as 'Consummation' ever be done if not for tortuous reasons? She thanked a Lord She scarcely believed in for the fact that such an act was against the laws of The City.

Then, there was a knock on Her door. It was The Guardians that were to lead The Woman and The Matron down to The Main Church for Her Pairing. The Matron informed them that they would be a few more minutes as they were still in Prayer, she then returned to the floor, beside The Woman. The Woman could see tears welling up in Her Matron's eyes. They did not seem like sad tears, however, but joyous ones. At that moment The Woman felt warm inside and smiled. She then listened patiently to The Matron as she finished her Prayer to The Lord Above.

Then, The Matron and The Woman embraced for the last time. They then rose and opened the door, greeting The Guardians, and the long walk to The Main Church began.

The Man's legs had begun to cramp and most of the pain had settled in His knees, which had rarely been reliable. He was used to that kind of pain and was able to stand there and wait. He showed no weakness or irritation towards the wait, but perhaps some boredom had shown through. He always seemed to be bored in Church and cared little for letting it show. It was a practice He had picked up long ago.

After a few more moments of standing and cramping, the doors to The Main Church finally opened and the fanfare He had expected began to sound. He leapt, slightly; jolted by the song He had never heard before as it began to play.

Then He saw Her. His chest became tighter than it had ever been as all the air He had left Him, instantly. Try as He might, He couldn't pull any air back in. The only thing He could do was gaze upon Her, in Her beautiful white tunic, as She walked down The Nave towards Him. All He could think of were Angels.

The Woman entered The Main Church with a flutter in Her chest. It was quelled quickly when She laid Her eyes upon Him. He was handsome. Not as handsome as Saul, mind you, but His eyes seemed gentle (if not bored) and His face was boyish, yet had distinct masculine features. He could use a haircut, that She could plainly see, but She liked that about Him. That coupled with His facial hair gave Him a rebellious spark. It was clear He'd shaved, but He'd left some hair on the sides of His face. That was not a direct infraction with the rules of Pairing Day, but it was clear by The Sermon Sayer's face that it was not smiled upon either.

She walked up to The Altar and met The Man who would be Her Partner. She took His extended hand. It was wet and warm. It was strange, yet not uncomfortable. She stood there, facing Him before The Sermon Sayer, who was holding The Book in his hands. She looked up at Her future Partner, and She decided then and there, that She liked Him, though She didn't know exactly why.

The Man smiled at The Woman who was smiling back at Him. He was getting lost in Her eyes and was having much difficulty getting through The Recitation of Vows, even though He had rehearsed them over and over again in the days leading up to The Service. He might've cared, if His future Partner had seemed to, but She did not. She just laughed at His foolishness, which made Him laugh at Himself, when He wasn't smiling at Her.

In fact, once He had seen Her, He couldn't stop smiling for some reason. He did not understand why He did so. He kept smiling, as did She all the way through The Service. They even kept smiling as They were lead back down The Nave, out of The Main Church, and taken to Their new compartment, which was located in The Complex of Peter, a more spacious complex than either of Them had known. It was located on the outskirts of The City, a fact which both of Them liked very much. It would be the first of many things that They would have in common.

II.

The Woman adored Their new compartment. It was more generous a gift than She'd expected The Pious Commonwealth to bestow upon Her and Her Partner. There was one large bedroom and a spacious living area. The washroom, unlike the ones They both were used to, was large and open. There was both a shower and a basin for washing. There was even a separate closet that wasn't located in the same room. She had it all mostly to Herself while The Man was at work, and She grew quite fond of learning about every nook and cranny.

She began to decorate the place almost immediately after settling in with Her Partner, who, She was pleased to discover, encouraged Her to do so. After a week's time it was looking like a place that She could be proud of, and how proud She was. Every Official Inspection, which happened twice a month, She would smile and greet The Inspectors, and always received the highest possible scores that could be given. It was something She could not brag about, however, for She feared a flogging for Pride and possibly even Vanity.

She found, in all that time of thought and reflection, that She feared most things about The Pious Commonwealth. The thought of their scorn stirred something inside of Her, a panic almost. At first, when She found Herself alone, She would manically double check Her actions and be sure that what She was doing strictly adhered to The Laws and Regulations of The Pious Commonwealth.

It had grown to be so consuming that one day Her new Partner had noticed Her nearly obsessive behavior and humorously chided Her for it. It was then She realized how foolish She'd been, and also when She realized how She felt about Her Partner.

She liked Him. She truly did. The only downside to Their Sacred Union was that He was a ritualistic flogger and, for the life of Her, She could not figure out why. He didn't seem like the type to adhere to the guidelines laid out for Him so reticently and it was the one conventional act He seemed to follow. It planted seeds of doubt in Her mind. She wanted Him to be trustworthy, but She could not bring Herself to trust Him fully. That is why She kept most of Her thoughts to Herself, especially those regarding The Pious Commonwealth.

The Man could not get Her out of His mind. To Him, She was wonderful. It began to affect His work. He was one of many Assistants to The Director of Nourishment, a job that required Him to make deliveries of food to the other Citizens across The City. However, from time to time, His homeward leaning thoughts caused Him to forget where exactly He was to deliver what.

After many weeks of that occurring, The Director himself had issued An Official Warning to The Man. It clearly stated that if The Man could not get His deliveries in order He would promptly be demoted to a poorer route with lesser pay. The Man laughed in the face of His Superior when He was given His Citation. He did not mean to, it had just come out.

After He'd received the flogging for Insubordination, The Man still felt The Director to be a foolish and pompous person who wrongly believed he had control over anyone. The Pious Commonwealth were the leaders here, not The Director. The Man felt it was almost Zealous to assume that anyone but them could hope for such control. Yet The Director did; he tried to rule with the iron fist reserved only for The One Above, and the fact that no one else saw that irked The Man to His very core. Despite all of that, The Man decided that He would forgive His Superior in an attempt to be more Christ-like.

He had found that He had a new outlook on life, which consisted of trying to be good to everyone (not even just the people He liked). There was a time when He would have found doing that difficult; in His old way of life He would be quick to anger and resentment, scorn and judgment. Quite honestly, He would lash out against anyone with whom He disagreed with. The new Him, however, shaped and changed by the short time He'd been with His Partner, saw the old way of living as a disagreeable way to carry yourself. He also realized that would draw unnecessary attention on Him and The Woman. Above all else, He didn't want Her falling under scrutiny because of Him. He liked Her far too much for that. She deserved to be treated well, both by The Pious Commonwealth and Him.

And He did treat Her well. Not because He felt He should, but because He couldn't help but do so. He knew that there was something incredibly extraordinary about Her. The time He spent with Her filled His chest with a warm feeling and Her radiance was a shower, washing Her glory over Him. The feeling She conjured up in Him reminded Him of a dream He had long ago and it was for that reason that He wanted to do something special for Her. After He built up the courage to do so, He inquired as to whether or not She would join Him for a visit to The Grand Hall of Gathering closest to Their new complex. To His elation, She agreed to The Man's proposal.

The Woman was nervous on the night of Their arrangement, yet She couldn't help but wear Her nicest tunic. She had never been to any of The Grand Halls before. She was especially excited because the one closest to Them had The River of Eden flowing through it. She had always wanted to see it and yet, Her nerves were getting the better of Her. It wasn't that She was afraid of alone time with Her Partner; that was something She had grown used to and fond of. What caused Her duress was that if someone were to see how They looked at each other, what would they think? Surely they'd think something was amiss with Them. Most Partners didn't stare at each other the way They did, nor did other Partners find any excuse to touch each other like They did. Their affection would surely be spotted if anyone had a watchful eye. Furthermore, She was absolutely positive that Her attire was too lavish for such a night; that is until She saw the look on His face when He walked in the door. She knew then that She looked just right.

Something overtook Them both in that moment and They came together as though They were pulled in to do so. It was the first time They embraced one another. Nothing had ever felt as right. They just stood there, in Their bedroom holding one another tightly, but not too tight. Then something peculiar happened.

For a moment, maybe even less than that, She felt something pressing up against Her leg from under His tunic. Before She could see what it was, The Man hastily excused Himself to the washroom to clean up for the night ahead of Them. She watched after Him and saw a look on His face as He went into the washroom. She tried to follow after Him, but He shut the door before She made it in. She stood there, outside of it, and listened. To Her chagrin, She could hear Him flogging Himself. She disliked when He did that, but He was very adamant about it. She didn't feel like it was Her place to interject over and over again. All She could ever do was sit there and listen and feel amiss and worry.

By the time The Man exited the washroom, The Woman had talked Herself out of Her worry. He smiled when He saw Her, looking clean and happy and rejuvenated. It caused Her heart to beat fiercely in Her chest. Unbeknownst to Her, when She smiled at Him it caused His heart to do the same.

Soon thereafter, They exited the compartment in haste, realizing They hadn't much time before The Sunset Bell rang. The sounding of The Bell made The Woman wonder for a moment about The Sun and The Moon as well. She wondered if She'd ever get to see them. She dared not bring it up to Her Partner, though. For some reason She felt guilty when She had thoughts like that. It was as though She possibly wasn't supposed to be having them. It wasn't Her place to question and wonder, yet it seemed to Her that was all She ever did.

The Man couldn't help but notice that She seemed distant and, if He were honest, He did not care for it. It made Him feel hollow and of little worth. There was also a speck of jealousy in His thoughts. He wished He could be in Her mind as much as She was in His, but that didn't seem to be the case very often. Her mind was a space only reserved for meaningful things and issues that were truly worthy of provoking thought. He knew She was an inquisitive soul and He knew He only breeched the surface of the inner-workings of Her mind most days. She would speak and it would be clear She was holding back for His benefit. He could tell She was afraid to say what was really on Her mind. Most of the time She could hold those thoughts at bay but many a night, even though They slept in separate beds, He could hear Her from across the room. Through a sleeping tongue She would murmur only one word:

Why?

Why, indeed. It was a powerful question, a question that would not leave His mind. He'd always been aware of the concept, but He could never give it a name. Not until She came into His life. Why should He do this? Why should He do that? Why was there this and not that? Why was He here and not there? Why was there now? Why was He unhappy until He met Her? Why? Why? Why? Why? Why could He not stop thinking about Why? Why could He not stop thinking about Her? Why was it that whenever She was in His presence He couldn't stop looking at Her?

As He gazed upon Her, studying every inch of Her face, He found Himself glad He did not have to work the next day. He told Himself that He would bring up the concept called Why then, so that They could discuss it fully. It was both a cause of excitement and anxiety as He was unaware of how He would begin that conversation. He quickly put that concern out of His mind, though. That was worth fretting over tomorrow. Today it was all about Her.

She was all that existed then. He barely even noticed the delicious supper They ate as They sat by The River of Eden. She was far too beautiful for Him to focus on anything else. He only looked away once, when The Woman made note of The River itself and its cool, crisp water that flowed though the man-made bends, cascading down the steady concrete incline. She told Him of how it was built to remind The Citizens of the outside world they once inhabited, before The Heathens ravaged that land and The Pious Commonwealth were forced to build The City. She commented on how awe-inspiring She found it all. The Man concurred, agreeing that it was awe-inspiring, but it was not quite as awe-inspiring as Her.

She smiled when He said that. He found Himself thinking of how He would gladly suffer a thousand floggings just to make Her smile again. Even just to hear Her speak. They discussed everything then, there by The River of Eden. She regaled Him with tales of The Crucifix, the large and ornate depiction of Christ on The Cross that hung high above Their heads, on the ceiling of The Grand Hall. To Him, it had merely just been a larger representation of The Crosses that hung in The Churches, offices, and compartments of the people here, granted with more attention paid to Christ's suffering. To Her, however it was a relic of times long ago. It used to hang in some great Church that had existed outside the walls of The City. She couldn't remember the specific place, but She assured Him it came from a different and, inferred by the way in which She said it, better time.

Once She was done speaking, nothing could make Him look away from Her. She noticed His gaze and He could tell, at first, it made Her uncomfortable. Then a small smile grew on Her face and in a playful manner She asked Her Question, the one He had only heard spoke from Her sleeping mouth. He couldn't help but smile as He answered Her. No one had ever thought to ask Him such a thing.

He told Her that it was because She was amazingly beautiful in every sense of the word. After He said that His smile continued on and She joined in. The two of Them smiled for the rest of the night. To The Man, that night, like The Woman, was perfect.

To say that The Woman was happy would be an understatement. On the way back to the compartment, She couldn't help but grab His hand and hold it in Her own. At first it seemed like such a strange impulse; She could see that it made Her Partner feel uncomfortable, but after a few steps They settled into the gesture and both of Them found They enjoyed it. They wondered why They had never done that before.

She then found Herself wondering why She had been inclined to do it at all. Why had She been compelled to act on that impulse of Hers? It was a question that bothered Her and one that She couldn't help but dwell on. Yet, had She known what other impulses She would soon act upon, She might not have thought about it with such fervor.

They soon arrived at Their home in what seemed like a short amount of time. When He opened the door for Her, Their eyes met, and She could see a tortuous look behind His. She could tell in that moment that He would excuse Himself to the washroom for a flogging soon. She had seen that look of unknown guilt on His face too many times to count in Their short time together. She could tell the night was pleasant for Him, but that He had over-thought it. Now His guilt was building and building. Why did He almost seem to insist on punishing Himself for nothing?

She did not want Him to go into that washroom. As soon as He closed the door behind Them, She turned to Him and, without much thought, did the first thing She could think of doing: She puckered Her lips slightly and gently pressed Her lips onto His. She held there for a moment and a wave of awkwardness washed over Her. It was quickly relieved when He returned Her passionate act with His own and pulled Her into Him by Her waist.

So They stood there, mouth-to-mouth, lips-on-lips, waist touching waist, in an embrace of utter infatuation. Soon, They began to open Their mouths to breathe and let each other's breath enter one another, which was soon followed, through some impulse unknown to Them, by Their tongues.

Their strange and foreign act seemed to go on for quite some time. The room swirled around Them. Their hands moved here and there. They touched. They felt, caressing. Then, seemingly out of nowhere, He stopped it all.

He held Her by the shoulders sternly and excused Himself to the bathroom, leaving Her standing there, confused and disappointed. She racked Her brain trying to think of what to do next, but the sound of His flogging made thinking difficult.

The Cleansing Rope stung with a lustrative burn as He brought it around, up over His head, and forced it to make contact with His bare back. He realized He was doing it much harder than He ever had before. The blood seemed to flow sooner than He was usually accustomed to. Yet, no matter how much force He put behind The Rope, He could not make the thoughts leave His mind. In fact, it seems to just exacerbate things.

Each lash seemed to bring all the thoughts He was trying to expel right to the forefront of His mind. He whipped and He thought. Images of Her body intertwined with His flashed with each flay and would not cease. Not even when His back grew numb and He felt no pain.

Finally, He gave up when exhaustion took over and He barely was capable of mustering up enough strength to climb onto the floor of the shower and turn it on. He rinsed the blood from His back with His remaining energy and then exited the shower, drying His wounds off gingerly.

When He entered the bedroom, He found His Partner in His bed waiting for Him. His first instinct was to ask Her to remove Herself, but before He could let out the command He saw the look in Her eyes. It was unmistakable. It was a look of wanting. As soon as He saw it He knew He felt the same way, it could not be denied. With that in His mind He climbed into bed with Her and They held each other close.

Lying there, in each other's arms for quite some time and despite the pain that was now creeping up His back, He felt a happiness He never imagined He could ever feel. She seemed to feel that way as well, it was evident by the smile on Her face. They drifted off to sleep that way, holding one another in bliss.

The Woman awoke the next day to an empty bed, and for a moment, She was saddened. She looked around, disoriented by Her new position in the room, but then She recalled and smiled. The smile did not hold on Her face long, however, for She heard the shower running.

She knocked before She entered the washroom. Her gentle rapping could not be heard over the sound of the running water, though. When She saw The Man, She could not help but stand there for a moment to take it all in. He was completely uncovered by cloth, and She had never seen anything more alluring. Yet, for some reason, She was nervous to enter further.

He took no notice of Her when She finally decided to approach the washbasin. She watched Him for a moment and then noticed the blood on the floor of the shower, whirling down the drain. Quietly, and after some deliberation about whether or not to disturb Him, She disrobed Herself and joined Him. As She slipped into the water, She touched Him tenderly and placed Her lips upon His self-inflicted wounds. At first touch, He jumped and turned sharply, startled, but then He saw Her and stood, embracing Her in His arms.

Their mouths then met again with more intensity and passion than the night before and soon She was pushed, ardently against the wall. She then felt something between Her legs; a part of Him She had yet to know. She felt a yearning for it. She needed it. Without a second thought She grasped it with Her hand, holding Him forcibly with desire. She placed the part of Him where Her water came from and with a soft moan from His lips He thrust into Her.

It was painful to Her at first and for a moment it seemed as though the tearing sensation might be too much for Her to bear. Yet, soon, even though the pain persisted, She let it continue on. The want for Him entirely was too great to stop.

The Man saw nothing but white beneath His shut eyes as He reached the apex of pleasure. He then opened His eyes and saw Her glowing face smiling at Him. He smiled back, basking in the euphoric feeling that was coursing through His body. The feeling would not last long, however, as a shadow seemed to cast itself into His field of vision and the darkness of reality swept back into His stream of consciousness. All of a sudden, He knew not what He had done and He knew not what He should do. All that He could think was that He needed to leave the shower. He needed to Cleanse.

Hurriedly and without thought, He went to where He kept The Cleansing Rope. The Rope was then hastily wrapped around His hand three times (as was His custom) and He dropped to His knees, closing His eyes in anticipation of what He was about to do. Before He could strike, however, He felt His Partner's touch upon His whipping hand.

He looked up to Her, still in the flesh, glistening and glowing. She looked like an Angel as Her sorrowful eyes met His. He tried to pull His hand away, to continue the duty He'd grown accustomed to doing when the feeling that consumed Him was all but inescapable, but She would not let Him go. She then pulled Him towards Her with a strength He did not know She had and rested His head upon Her chest. At first He struggled, but then, after a moment of hesitation, He found it oddly soothing.

She then asked Her Question and it struck Him like a blow to the gut. He had never contemplated why He used The Cleansing Rope before. When He tried to think of it, a realization came over Him:

There was no real reason for Him to Cleanse.

When that dawned on Him, He felt a warmth move through His body; a tingling sensation that caused His skin to rise into little bumps. It started in His chest, then moved to His throat, it flashed up His face, and then came out of His eyes in streams of water. He'd never known that feeling before. It was a feeling of release with some sorrow and joy mixed in. It was something He'd only known from reading about it in The Book, but He never thought it possible to feel such a thing.

He wept, letting everything out; the happiness He'd hidden, the sorrow He'd kept inside, the guilt of feeling at all, and the hatred of letting guilt consume Him. All of it just flooded out of His eyes as His head laid upon His Partner's bare chest.

Once He had let it all out and calmed Himself, She helped Him up and in to Their bedroom where She laid Him down on Their bed. She then lay down beside Him in Her small, yet strong, arms and He noticed He felt at peace. So there, after lying in bed with Her for some time in peaceful silence He decided it was a good time to talk to Her about the concept of Why.

At first The Woman felt embarrassed. She was unaware that She spoke while in slumber, but He reassured Her that it was not a nuisance or a bother, which made Her feel slightly better. He then inquired as to what reason She talked in Her sleep at all. What was it that compelled Her to utter that word from Her dreams? She answered Him truthfully: She did not know. She had always been that way, always dissatisfied, always yearning for more. She found Herself asking that question quite a bit in Her mind and She supposed that in Her sleep She did not have the self-control She possessed in Her waking life.

They then spoke for hours about this and that and everything in between. They laughed and cried and shouted and whispered and came to several realizations about Themselves, Their situation, and The Pious Commonwealth. At first They submitted Their accusations against the current state of Their lives in a hushed, unsure tone, but when They realized

They were both speaking from the same state of mind, They spoke with confidence and concurrence.

Even still, despite how well the conversation They were having was unfolding, The Woman was uncertain as to whether or not She should tell Her Partner what Her most closely guarded theory was. However, after a few more back-and-forths, when She found She had confessed other things that inevitably lead up to Her secret way of thought, She felt it was the right time. She told Him what She thought.

She did not believe in the same Higher Power as The Pious Commonwealth. To Her there was no singular omnipotent being responsible for everything the two of Them had ever known, but rather, something else: A deep presence that ebbed and flowed through the lives of anyone and everyone, leaving everybody connected. She acknowledged that Her concept had spawned from some passages in The Book, but The Book was also riddled with inconsistencies of the supposedly unfaultable Creator.

Her Partner found Her undeniably adorable as She explained Her viewpoint. She would backtrack often, fearing that perhaps He did not see the things She saw in the same light. He would reassure Her that everything was okay and would listen as She kept going. Finally She reached the end of Her thought and smiled nervously at Him. The smile turned confident when She saw Him smile back.

Her Partner then asked Her how She knew all of that. She found the answer was simple: She had always known it. It was the same sense of knowledge that caused Her to act upon Her urges the night prior and the current morning. Now, more than ever, She knew it to be undeniably true. She was confident in Her explanation, more confident then She'd been all day, yet She found that She was filled with a strange kind of regret when She finished speaking and a silence fell upon the room.

The Man looked up at the ceiling for a few moments, processing what had just been said to Him. All of those ideas were notions that He Himself had entertained at one point or another, but when they escaped those beautiful lips of Hers, they became a real, almost palpable thing. He could no longer deny these thoughts in His head. It wasn't a private thought anymore. It was a communal one. It was also a thought that, in His mind at least, proved the very concept They had been discussing. He looked at Her in disbelief for a few moments (it seemed like an eternity to Her) and then He told Her how He felt and They both laughed. He then realized, as He hoped She had too, that the two of Them were brought to one another by a force They had both separately discovered together.

He embraced Her and She embraced Him back. Their lips met again. She then placed Him where She wanted Him and He entered Her as He had before. They fully embraced there in the bed, in bliss and satisfaction. When They had found euphoria together, He discovered that He lacked the compulsion to leave Her. He stayed lying there, inside Her, still as one. After some time in that peaceful, tranquil, euphoric state of silence He began to notice that a stinging pain began to creep up His back. He left Her and sat up on the edge of the bed and reached around to feel where the pain was coming from. When He reached His hand back around to the front, He saw the light catch the red of blood that coated His fingers. His wounds appeared to have reopened.

Softly She cooed and grabbed His hand with Hers, examining the blood, before She examined His back.

He knew what was to come next. She asked again why He had done what He had done to Himself.

When He'd heard Her Question for a second time, He realized that She was surely due an explanation. A true explanation. It took Him awhile to find the words to explain it to Her. That it was a trait that had been bred in to Him by His Rearers and even though He had mastered the art of not caring what anyone thought, He had not mastered the art of not feeling guilty about not caring. That guilt, as strange as it was, would wrap its clawed hands around His neck like a demon He'd been told about in Church. The Man explained that the flogging relieved the guilt, but not the Sin, so if He thought about a Sin again, the guilt would return full force.

It was then, after He'd given His convoluted explanation, that He realized the errors of His ways. Flogging was not a solution, but rather a hindrance. He would need to come to terms with the fact that His guilt spawned from the concepts of other people regarding Sin, not His own. The Man would need to define His own right and wrong. He especially would need to figure out a way to deal with any guilt He may feel, from that point forward, in a manner that did not invoke self-harm.

As He thought that aloud, He knew it would be difficult. Retraining His brain to think correctly would not be an easy task. It could possibly take years to undo the damage His Rearers and The Pious Commonwealth had done. The thought of the time it would take to prevail over His inner turmoil seemed daunting and overwhelming. It made Him feel slightly depressed about the whole ordeal. Then She rubbed His face.

She held Him in Her hands and looked The Man in the eyes, vowing to help Him with the grand mission He was about to endure. She reassured Him that He would not be alone. The Man looked at The Woman for some time, not knowing whether She was being honest and true, but He did not need to look very long to discern that She was, in fact, sincere. He smiled with joy and thanked Her with all of His heart.

As She washed the blood from His back and whispered sweet things into His ears, She could tell He had grown tired. She Herself was exhausted. She knew it was late for The Sunset Bell had rung long ago and the lights in the corridor outside Their compartment had been dimmed for hours. They had talked about everything and in doing so the day had passed Them by. It did not matter, though, because to Her it was worth it.

Once He was clean, She dried Him off, dabbing gently around His wounds with the softest towel They owned. He hugged Her and thanked Her for Her tenderness when She was done. She smiled at Him and led Him to Their bedroom by the hand.

They were both still in Their bare flesh when They entered the room, and commented on how They hadn't dressed all day. They hurried under the linens of His bed and She moved Herself close to Him, laying Her hand upon His chest and watching as it moved up and down with His breathing. She listened to the slow and steady thumps that were caused by His heart.

Before They drifted off to sleep, She whispered to Him how glad She was to have been Paired with Him. He reciprocated the notion and whispered three magnificent and powerful words to Her. She liked hearing them in His voice. They were words that She had only heard uttered to the ceiling of The Churches by The Sermon Sayers and The Matrons.

Her mind fluttered off to sleep that night, while She was smiling all the while. That night She dreamed of being in better places and better times. All with Him, of course.

III.

Two years had crept up on Him. He was unprepared for the day at hand. When He pressed Himself to think about it, He knew He had kept the day in His mind. He had pushed it back, though; far from the consciousness He used every day. Most of His time had been spent working or with His Partner. He had grown accustomed to living the way They did. He adored the moments with Her and enjoyed the thoughts He would have at work while She was at home keeping the compartment in order. He did not want anything, or anyone (as it were), forcing itself into His life and ruining everything He held dear. So when The Guardians came to escort Them to The Main Church, His heart sank a bit as His mind raced with the fears of what was to come.

Yet, He needed only to look at Her to see He was being foolish for thinking that something as life-changing as the ritual They were about to undertake would ever cause a schism to grow between Them. He squeezed Her hand quickly, out of the sight of

The Guardians, and then They were lead towards The Main Corridor. As They walked, He would candidly glance over His shoulder at Her. He could see that there was worry on Her face. He could tell, just by Her expression, that it was not the same worry He had known. He disliked it all the same, however. All He wished to do was to comfort Her with His arms or, better yet, His lips, but displays of affection in public were quite frowned upon and the last thing They needed was The Pious Commonwealth breathing down Their necks.

When They finally arrived at The Church, The Guardians opened the grand door for Them. He ushered Her in before Him, placing His hand gently on Her back. He hoped it would be enough comfort to Her for the time being, but He knew He was hoping in Vain. The look on Her face hid the dread She had for the upcoming ceremony from everyone else but Him.

They walked briskly down The Nave, towards The Altar. Both of Them wanted to put what was happening in Their pasts as quickly as possible. It was like something in Them thought that if They got through it with haste then it would cease from happening altogether.

She took Her place, kneeling by The Altar and He walked up and joined Her. Then The Sermon Sayer entered from the side of The Church and greeted Them both fondly, as if he'd known Them all Their lives. The Man knew that to be a lie, for He'd never seen that particular Sermon Sayer before. Still, He smiled and greeted him back, even if He was cursing the charlatan in His mind.

The Sermon Sayer then began The Ceremony, reading the passages and reciting the rites. Then he looked down at The Man and asked Him to swear On High, which The Man did, vacantly. He did nothing On High anymore. His services and allegiances were offered only to Her.

When The Child that would be Theirs was brought out to Them, kneeling by The Altar, The Woman felt nothing. To Her, It was nothing more than another chore that The Pious Commonwealth was forcing upon Her. Chores were something She did not have time for anymore. She had the luxury of not being Paired with a man who had respect for rules and rituals. Instead of playing the normal role of a female Partner (preparing the meals, keeping the compartment tidy, making sure her male counterpart was taken care of so he could perform his duties at work, etc.) She was able to ignore all the duties bestowed on women under The Pious Commonwealth and focus on other things, such as Her Passions.

Her Partner had hidden a writing utensil in His tunic at work one day and brought it home as a gift for Her. She was excited when She received it and couldn't wait to discover all of the uses it had. She began by writing. Poems in the beginning, just verses of words She found beautiful strung together in a manner She found appealing. She dedicated each one to Her Partner and would read them to Him somewhat sheepishly when He returned home each day. He seemed to enjoy them very much and that inspired Her to write more and more and more.

Soon from poetry, She moved to prose. She would write tales of The Heathens and of the world before The Pious Uprising. Unlike how they were told to Her, She would write of The Heathens fondly and showed favor to the characters that were normally portrayed as villains. She would write from their point-of-view and there was something quite exciting about it.

Then She found the utensil had other uses: She began to use it to draw. She cherished that act so. As a child, She had done it with such excitement but had somehow lost the ability, as She grew older. She rediscovered Her forgotten talent one day while mindlessly moving the utensil about on a page. While She was pondering how Her next verse should begin, She drew a face. It was a clumsy depiction, to be sure, but a face could be seen nonetheless. She then felt She should pursue that task and perfect it, so that She could bring pictures in Her mind onto the parchment. With practice She graduated from crude representations to realistic portraits and artistry of an absurd nature. That paved the way for Her attempt at making replicas. She would craft little palaces and homes that She'd imagined out of bits and pieces of things She had acquired from here and there.

She had grown to adore these forms of expression. It had become a way to escape living life in The City. Yet now, as She stared at The Child in front of Her, She knew that being with It was the new present and that all of Her artistry now laid in the past.

At least The Child seemed well behaved. She had to give It credit for that. Horror stories had been passed around all women about screaming babies and

Rearers who could not bring them satisfaction. She was pleased that didn't appear to be the case with Her and The Child. It even stayed calm through The Baptism, a task that She Herself was not able to accomplish. It was a tale Her own Rearers enjoyed telling and retelling over and over again.

As She thought about how tortuous that must have been for Her Rearers, The Sermon Sayer handed The Little One to Her and She looked down at It. Their eyes met and there was a brief moment in time where something She could not explain transpired. She would be mistaken if She'd said She felt nothing, yet still, as She stood there with The Child in Her arms, She felt as if a heavy weight had been placed upon Her.

The Man and His Partner's duties there were completed and so They traveled home with The Child bestowed upon Them. The Guardians escorted Them through the corridors. If they had not been there, He would have offered to carry The Little One, as It seemed to be a heavy load for Her to bear alone. It was a task that would have seemed out of place, however, and for that reason He resented The Pious Commonwealth quite fiercely; they seemed to have an animosity towards compassion between Partners.

Once They were home, comfort washed over Him as He watched The Guardians retreat down the corridor. He closed the door to the compartment and turned to His Partner immediately and laid His lips upon Hers. He found it strange now, what with being in the presence of The Child. It watched Them with Its eyes so intently. They parted Their embrace awkwardly.

They decided to place It on the floor and sit in the chairs of the living area, watching The Little One grow accustomed to Its new surroundings. There, They observed the new member of Their household as It crawled about, playing with the little trinkets that had been brought for It by the Convocation of Rearers earlier that day (when the crib had been delivered).

They discussed in hushed tones what They were expected to do with It. Neither of Them came to any conclusions or found any solutions that satisfied Them. As They talked The Woman couldn't take Her eyes off The Little One. She seemed wary of The Child on the floor. The Man was a little more at ease with It than She. It crawled up to Him several times and played with the bottom of His tunic, which had little strings perfect for pulling that had frayed off with wear and age. Yet, despite the innocent gesture, The Child made Him feel awkward, and He knew not what to do in the situation He currently found Himself in.

They continued to deliberate about The Child for hours, His Partner and He, yet no plan would come into fruition. They finally agreed, after The Sunset Bell had sounded, that They should put The Child in Its crib and settle down for the night.

The Woman lay there with The Man and just stared at The Child in Its crib. She watched, sleeplessly, as It familiarized Itself with the new place It was expected to sleep in. It crawled around a bit, pushing Itself with Its legs and bracing Itself with Its arms. It moved in little circles for sometime, clearly tying to figure out what sort of contraption It was in.

Then The Little One hoisted Itself up, using Its little fingers to grip the surrounding frame and supported Itself on the edge of the crib. It took a long look around the room and then, after a few moments, It let Itself plop down, onto the bedding. After a few moments more, The Child let Itself fall fast asleep and was snoring gently.

Then a strange thing happened. As It slept, She found She couldn't help but watch It sleep. She let Her mind ponder Its existence. She wondered where The Little One came from. Of course She knew that all children were held in The Nursery in The Complex of Mary until they were at least one year of age. Then, from there, they were assigned to Rearers. Even though She knew all of that, She couldn't help but wonder about where they could've come from before that.

From a very young age, She'd known of the concept of Birth and knew that only women could do it. Birth was another purpose for where She made water from. She was unaware of the specifics though, and that's what caused Her to rack Her mind at that moment. How did the children get in there?

She had a certain feeling, a notion really, brought on by a churning in Her gut that tickled and wiggled, almost. From that feeling She concocted an idea that it all might have something to do with what Her and Her Partner did from time to time when Their passion for each other needed to be expressed in a physical form. Unfortunately, as much as She liked that theory, She wrote it off because She knew that it could not be proven or disproven because The Pious Commonwealth bestowed Impotence on males and made it so females were Barren from Birth.

Then, She thought that perhaps She shouldn't write it off so quickly; perhaps something could be done to prove it. After all, Her Partner had overcome Impotence, maybe it would not be so difficult for Her to overcome being Barren.

Clearly women who weren't Barren had to exist. Non-Barren women had to be responsible for the gift of life for Their sleeping Child and others like It. She just could not fathom where in The City they could be located. Perhaps they too were in The Complex of Mary as well? If that were so, then did they rear the children until The Rearers took over? Are they sad when their children are taken from them? Or do they never get to meet them?

It seemed as though each question She tried to answer only provided more questions. She fell asleep that night with Her eyes on The Child. Her mind was spinning around, with thoughts of It.

The Man had begun to busy Himself with His work. Not because He believed in it, mind you, but because it was all He could do to not dwell on what He would do when He returned home to His Partner and The Child. Before the arrival of It, He would come home and just get to be with Her. Most nights They would speak with one another deeply, conversing about topics ranging from Morality to Faith (both of which They had redefined, making the meanings Their own, rather than that of The Pious Commonwealth). Other nights, They would laugh and joke and He would marvel at the newest piece of art She'd created before She tucked them away in Her special hiding place that The Inspectors could not find. Some nights, however, They would let passion take over and caress each other and touch lips and other such things. All of those nights were behind Them now.

All The Child was to Him was another pair of eyes, watching and judging Him. He couldn't speak in a radical nature or find the urge to be passionate. The Child's eyes were the eyes of The Pious Commonwealth and He couldn't be Himself in front of It.

That was having horrible effects on Him. When He couldn't be Himself - When He couldn't express what

He was feeling - that is when the guilt would begin to set back in and when it set back in it would build. It was growing to be quite large in His mind now and even began to creep through the rest of His body. To His hands that itched for The Cleansing Rope and His back that craved a sting. He was worried these sensations would give way to impulse soon enough and He would find Himself flogging again. It was a fear He wanted to talk about, yet He could not voice it to His Partner, for The Child was always around.

He began to feel as though He was going mad with desperation and worry. Rather than dwell on it, He would just focus on His deliveries, making sure stock was up and that everything was getting to where it was supposed to be in a timely manner. It was the most productive He had ever been. He did not know how to feel about that.

The Woman had tried to welcome The Child into Her heart, She really had, but She found it very difficult to do so. She resented The Little One for the distance She felt growing between Her Partner and Herself. On top of that, It also created excess work for Her. It was always getting into things, reaching into the nooks and crannies of the compartment, causing messes in Its wake. On top of that It would soil Itself regularly and required changing, a task She dreaded constantly.

Yet for all the grief It caused Her, The Child never really cried. There was an occasional whine, when It wanted food or sleep or to be put in clean clothes, but She never heard It wail in the way She had been warned about. That was something She appreciated about The Child.

Even though The Child didn't cry, sometimes She did. Whenever She found a moment alone (or alone enough), She would go to the bathroom and lock the door and let the tears flow out. It was only for a moment, for She didn't want to leave The Child alone for long (even if It was asleep), but She wept for Her lost passions; the ones shared with Her Partner in those special moments of bliss and the others She shared with Herself and Her utensil and Her parchment. The words and thoughts and pictures all whirled and twisted around in Her head, building themselves up with no outlet and turning themselves into frustrations. That's how She was feeling at that moment: frustrated.

She was busy battling that bout of dissatisfaction,

while washing the disgusting stains out of The Little One's tunic, when it dawned on Her that She had not seen The Child in some time. She quickly turned around and scanned the room, but It was nowhere to be found. She frantically began to search under things, knowing The Child liked to hide, but It wasn't in the spots It usually frequented. So She made Her way into the bedroom and looked under the beds and the crib.

It seemed as if The Child had vanished completely and panic began to take hold of Her. Her breath quickened, as did the beating of Her heart. She sat upon the bed and tried to get Her thoughts together, trying to think of what to do. In silence, She sat there, with no idea of where else to look. It was then that She heard a rather strange noise.

It was a small scratching noise. Faintly it could be heard resounding off the stone walls of the compartment. She quickly stood, trying to discern where the noise was coming from. She moved here and there, attempting to pinpoint it's origin. Eventually, Her quest led Her to the closet by the bathroom.

She opened the door and moved the tunics along the

back wall, over to the side. There, in Her secret hiding spot, the place where all the treasures She had created were kept, sat The Child. Her utensil was in Its hand and The Little One was moving it around and around on a piece of blank parchment that had been stored there. Without thought, She grabbed The Child and the parchment, assuming The Child was wasting the utensil on meaningless things. She gently scolded It.

Then She looked at the parchment.

It was beautiful. Simple, yes, yet She could not help but look past the crudeness of the shapes and lines to the meaning of The Child's actions. Their Child had created something, all on Its own. That was a feat even She wasn't sure She could accomplish until a little less than two years ago. She knew then, there was something special about The Child.

What She experienced then was a bittersweet moment. She was overjoyed at the fact She could share something with The Child, but here, in The City, creativity was to be wiped away. At that moment in time She realized the potential of The Child and that, among The Pious Commonwealth, It could never thrive.

The Man had held off long enough and decided to cease working and return to His compartment for the evening. It was a long walk back to His home, made even longer by the fact He stood outside the door for quite some time before He entered.

He froze, standing there for a moment, taking it all in. He almost could not believe what He was seeing. His Partner was dozing there, on the chair in the living area, Her utensil and parchment in hand. The Child was sitting on the floor in front of Her playing with a little wooden block with the depiction of Christ on it. The Man watched The Child for some time before He came back to reality and shut the door quickly behind Him, before anyone could peek in and see.

The Little One, who had been so enthralled with Its toy block, had Its attention drawn to The Man by the sound of the shutting door. Then, The Child did something truly wonderful. It threw the block of Christ on the floor and proceeded to prop Itself up on Its legs. Before that moment, The Child usually had to brace Itself on something to stand, but this time It stood there, all on Its own, balancing clumsily. Then It took a step. Then another. And another. It did that, step after step, until It had reached The Man. The only thing The Man could do is watch in awe as The Child walked to Him and then, with a clumsy kind of grace, embraced His leg with Its pudgy little arms.

The embrace He received was not the same kind of embrace He shared with His Partner, but it was similar in a way. He could feel an emotion coarse through Him that He had previously only associated with Her. He reached down to The Child and picked It up, looking The Little One in the eyes. In that moment The Child took a place in The Man's heart, and it made Him feel warm and happy.

Then, after He and The Child shared a moment, a moment in which He saw within It an inner beauty that He had missed before, He began to feel sorry for The Little One. Inner beauty could not survive in The City. He knew not what to do for It. He looked over to His Partner, who had silently woken at some point during His realization and He could tell that She knew what He was thinking. She felt the same way as Him. They then just looked at each other for a very, very long time.

Neither of Them wanted Their Child to have the lives They had led.

IV.

The Woman embraced The Man one more time before He left for work and held Their Child up so that It could say goodbye as well. The Child had grown quickly over the past few months, and it seemed like It was growing larger with each passing day. It had even begun speaking in little words and broken sentences. It would light up Her Partner's face when Their Child spoke to Him, but today was different, behind the smile She could see the stress in His eyes.

A Messenger of The Commonwealth had visited Them the night prior, just before The Sunset Bell rang, and delivered unto Them a note directly from The Director of Nourishment, requesting a meeting with Her Partner. The letter had troubled Him. It seemed to come without notice. Her Partner knew it could not be good; every meeting He'd ever had with The Director had not been a pleasant one, not a single one had ever even come close to being cordial.

He gave Her one last, almost pitiful glance before He left Their compartment and shut the door behind Him. She worried for Him. Not because of what He might be asked to do, but because of what He might do if the meeting did not go the way He wanted it. She didn't want Him to start flogging again. She had seen the thought cross His face many times since the arrival of the summons. It wasn't just self-harm that She worried about, either.

Recently, He had grown increasingly radical in thought. It was the presence of Their Child and the effect It had on the both of Them that caused something to wake within Him. The Little One seemed special, and They both feared that if It grew up the way They had, that Its magnificence and uniqueness, the whimsy It inspired, would all be squandered. When It came out of the machine that was The Pious Commonwealth's City, It would be nothing more than a plain, wooden block, like the very toys It played with. By the end of it all, The Little One would be just like everyone else. Both Her and Her Partner concurred that They did not want that for It.

The only problem worthy of note was that it would be impossible for The Child to grow up any other way. With that realization had come a mighty frustration. The Man had talked to Her about going as far as joining The Zealots, a radical group with an ironic name, and their underground plot to overthrow The Pious Commonwealth. Despite Her objections, He went so far as to try and make contact with the band of rebels. Fortunately, for Her, He failed before He even started when He realized that He did not know the first place to look for them. The Woman wondered if they even existed at all or if they were just tools used to invoke fear, like Beelzebub or any of the other demons The Pious Commonwealth taunted the masses with. Just the same to Her, She was relieved when His plan did not go through. Still She worried, because that spark that had lit inside Him seemed like it would not extinguish itself.

She could not worry then, however, and The Child seemed to know it as well, for It had already ventured to the back of Their closet and started grabbing the supplies It and Its Rearer would use to expand Their minds. The Woman always smiled when She would watch It fumble with the utensil and parchment and bring it up to Her for Her approval, which She would always give. She would smile even more once She set up the parchment on Their little table. She let The Little One draw whatever It wanted.

The Woman had taught It to draw, almost immediately after She discovered Its incredible want to learn. She hesitated on teaching Their Child to write, however, for She feared if It excelled too quickly in school, then suspicions would be aroused. If that were to happen, She was certain that things would not end well for It, or even Them. The Pious Commonwealth seemed to despise knowledge and intelligence, and She wanted their Wrath as much as She wished to be a pillar of salt.

The Director of Nourishment, in all his esteemed glory, had called it a promotion, yet The Man knew it was not so. He knew He was being punished for something. His heart was simply not in His work any longer and, despite much presentation, He knew His animosity had shown through at one time or another. He simply could not bring Himself to care any longer. Not with a wonderful Partner and an aspiring Child at home. He knew that is why He found Himself here.

His new assignment was to deliver food to The Complex of Judas, or The Unholy Complex as it was colloquially known. It was a special complex where all the undesirables were moved to and closely watched. It was home to members of The Zealots that had been captured, Hellions, Charlatans, Murderers, and The Seven Deadly Sinners (although, The Man would not be delivering food to The Annex of Gluttony for they received special rations of food and had proved time and time again they could not be trusted around the food cart). Every now and then, The Unholy Complex would sometimes get a hold of a Heathen or two whenever one had decided to breach The City's walls for one allegedly nefarious reason or another.

At first, The Man actually thought nothing of His new assignment. Truth be told, He was even a little glad when He first heard the news. Then it had dawned on Him that He would be working with undesirables, which meant that He Himself could be considered undesirable. It made Him worry that maybe The Pious Commonwealth knew something about Him. Suspicion crept up His neck as He entered The Unholy Complex on the day He was to begin working there.

As He was escorted through the grand door for the first time, The Guardians of The Unholy warned Him of a few things He might encounter. He was informed of the horrors He would probably witness, of the men He would come across, and of the rules

He must follow if He wished for Himself and The City to remain safe. He was warned against fraternizing with any of The Sinners, as some of them, especially The Zealots, were quick talkers who would prey on sympathy or weakness with dishonesty and mistrust. He was not to talk to anyone and they warned Him that He would be watched. To clarify their sentiment, they motioned up to the large black orbs that hung from the ceiling that reminded The Man of emotionless, evil eyes that might belong to a demon.

The final warning they gave Him was that He was to beware The Heathen. They had discovered Him breaking in to The City and threw Him into a cell immediately. They claimed He was a savage and that He would use any means necessary to escape. The Man was instructed to keep His guard up at all times.

As He set about His work, He thought The Guardians of The Unholy that had warned Him were just being petty and childish. The Man had found that The Sinners in the complex were of little threat to Him or anyone really. In fact, He discovered Himself seeing them as just normal individuals. None of them seemed demonic or transformed by Sin. They were all just normal human beings. Just like

Him.

The Woman was in the midst of teaching The Child how to draw The Sun or, as it were, Her interpretation of an interpretation of a symbol that She saw in a picture book a long time ago. It was nothing more than a circle with lines distending from it, giving it the look of light. The Woman found Herself wishing She had a colored writing utensil. She remembered The Sun, as it had been depicted, had been yellow, or perhaps orange. It really had been a long time ago. For some reason She felt that orange would have sufficed after all, but then She wished She had yellow again. She didn't know why orange had suddenly popped in Her head. Perhaps She was recalling a memory of another picture from another book from another time.

She decided not to dwell on what She did and did not have and instead continued to instruct The Little One. The Woman began, as The Child watched, to draw something She knew to be The Moon. It was a simple little figure to draw; two curved lines that connected at the top and bottom, one inside the other.

Once She finished The Moon, She began to draw a Star, but then She stopped. The Star (as She knew how to depict it) was banned, outright, by The Pious Commonwealth for The Hellions use of it in their pentagrams. She looked over to The Child, who had already begun trying to copy The Moon drawing from The Woman's parchment.

The Woman, for some reason, could not get the image of The Moon out of Her mind. All She could see was a purple and blue sky, The Moon there, large and off to the side. Stars were strewn all about. The night scene They were drawing would be nothing with just The Moon. So She just drew a Star and another and another, knowing full well that She would have to hide these drawings very well. She might even have to burn them.

It took The Man only a few weeks to learn the complete layout of The Complex of Judas. He soon knew it like the back of His hand. He actually enjoyed His new job. It was a smaller delivery area with fewer people in it, which meant it was a shorter route all together. That, coupled with the lack of small talk, meant that He would often be done early, which meant more time at home with His Partner and

Their Child. It was a priceless perk of the job, which He adored greatly.

He had found Himself smiling more here, among the degenerates, than He ever did when He had delivered food to the people in the other complexes. He couldn't explain why, but He actually liked it here. There was less false modesty and judgment from the men and women in the cells. No one here believed him- or herself to be better than anyone else, nor did they feel the need to compete with others for foolish reasons no one really understood. It was simpler there without all the hypocrisy.

However, there were parts of His new job that He did not like. Such as delivering food to the area that The Hellions resided in. They adored the occult and worshipped The Dark One himself. Despite the fact The Man did not believe in any of that nonsense, their imagery frightened Him so. Their shouts and calls also struck a chord with Him, for they were mean and threatening, not just to Him, but to His Family as well. He had been mistaken for one of the cogs of The Pious Commonwealth's machine, and they didn't care for those types in here. However, He was able to take solace in the fact that The Hellions could never make good on their threats against His life because they would never, ever be let out.

Aside from The Hellions, the rest of His rounds were easy. Granted, He was greeted with temptation from time to time, mainly from The Zealots, who would call to Him from their cells and beg Him to sneak letters or messages or other paraphernalia back and forth between the other complexes. They would beseech Him with any means they could. Most times they just yelled to Him of their innocence, as if He were The Grand Judge himself. The only thing that might make Him consider helping any of them would be if they promised Him an audience with a Zealot on the outside, but none ever did. He thought about inquiring about it Himself, but all He needed to do is look up at those ominous, dark orbs and those notions would be quashed. Those constantly creepy, demon-like eyes were enough for Him to walk the straight and narrow, and so He would put His head down and continue on His route, silently cursing that He couldn't bring down The Pious Commonwealth once and for all.

His days would often end with The Sinners. He would make His way down each corridor, giving the food parcels out to The Envious and The Greedy. Some days, The Slothful couldn't be bothered to collect their parcels, and The Man could just continue on His route. He liked whenever that would happen. It sped up the day for Him.

The last Sinners on His route were The Lustful, whores and rapists alike. He would enter with His cart and slide their little parcels through the bars. Some would thank Him; others would just take their food and go back to their cot. Others still, would show Him what was under their tunics or they would try to grab a hold of Him to see what was under His. Thankfully, He was quick on His feet.

Although, one day, while slipping a parcel to a man accused of whorish acts, The Whore grabbed The Man's wrist and pulled Him close to his cell. All The Man could do was listen as The Whore hurled accusation after accusation upon Him. The Whore claimed that The Man was no better than he, and that The Whore could see it on His face and smell it from His lap. The Whore said everyone could see it and soon, The Man would be thrown in there, with him, and Impotence would be forced into Him, again and again, until the needs He and The Whore shared were gone forever.

The Man violently twisted His hand free after some

time of struggle. Once He was free, all He could do was stare at The Whore as he went on and on about knowing The Man and he were similar. Surely, The Whore was an insane person, driven mad by the acts he committed, or perhaps the acts committed against him in The Complex of Judas. The Man could plainly see that something was not right with The Whore, but what if he spoke some semblance of truth?

The Man looked up at the all-seeing black orb, and a fear He'd never felt so intensely trickled down His spine like water so cold it burns.

The Woman grew nervous as She listened to The Man's tale. He had begun telling it almost as soon as He entered the door to Their compartment that night. She could not believe what She was hearing. How could The Whore have known? Was it that obvious? Were Her and Her Partner really not hiding what They've been doing very well? If that were the case, the consequences could be dire.

It was evident that The Man was in no mood to converse about it after He'd told Her the story. Instead, They just sat with internalized emotions and played with Their Child. That always seemed to change His mood. They would normally wrestle about and roll around the compartment for hours, laughing all the while. She would be able to visibly see His stress dissolve away. Yet today, She could plainly see, that would not be the case.

Despite His laughter and joy at hoisting Their giggling Child above His head, She knew today's problem would not go away with ease. It was apparent to Her because every time He looked up from The Little One to Her, His expression would change, if even for an instant, from one of happiness to one of deep concern. She could see the worry was stuck with Him tonight.

The worry transferred to Her too, as She watched Them from Her chair. All She could think of was what would happen if He were taken from Them? Would They be able to visit Him? Would The Pious Commonwealth take Her as well? That was perhaps the most unsettling thought of all: What if Their Child was taken away from Them? It would surely be assigned to another set of Rearers, to be raised by someone less qualified than She. Its ambitious spirit would be stomped down and then where would It be? The spark in Its soul would certainly be snuffed and the possibility of what It could become would be lost forever. She knew She could not let that happen, but She didn't know exactly what to do. It was something that She pondered for the rest of the evening.

Later in the night, after They supped and put Their Child down for Its slumber, She joined Her Partner in the shower. She thought They might speak of the looming dread She felt in Her chest, yet when it came time for Them to open Their mouths to speak, They both could not find the right words to express Themselves. Instead, They met lips and felt each other with Their hands. Soon, He had entered Her and They were one yet again. To Her, it felt different, it was still sweet and passionate, yet there was a certain somberness that hung over Their heads as They committed the once joyous act. Then it dawned on Her: it seemed as though They might be doing it for the last time.

At work, the day after the incident with The Whore, The Man was relieved to discover that He and His Partner might have been overly presumptuous. Nothing had been said to Him, and no one looked at Him as suspiciously as He imagined they would. He was free to go about His work in peace.

There was still tension, though, and each time He passed one of The Guardians of The Unholy He couldn't help but look away. The thought of making eye contact with one of them made His stomach drop. He knew it looked suspicious, but suspicions would have been far worse had they been able to look into His eyes and see that He was hiding something. He found that it was easier if He just went about His rounds while staring at His feet.

That, as it happened, made the day go by quickly and before He knew it He was in the corridor that housed The Murderers. With His mind busy trying to be inconspicuous, it was easy to drown out the incessant wails of insanity and repentance coming from the cells of the stabbers and stranglers as He passed them their food through the bars. When He was done there, He moved on to His next stop, the corridor that contained just one prisoner.

The hall reserved for The Heathens was usually vacant, but for the past several weeks one man had occupied it. He had, apparently, been caught in the ceiling attempting to steal food from the people of The Complex of Paul. On the first few days of The Man's employment in The Unholy Complex, The Heathen had been like the rest of the captured and begged Him for freedom. The Heathen went on and on about his family on the outside of the walls of The City and how he needed to see them, desperately; he even apologized to The Man for spying on The City and vowed never to do it again. The Man just needed to let him go. All The Heathen wanted was to get out of The City as quickly as possible, he said as much himself, fear added a shakiness to his voice. The Man had said nothing to The Heathen and just passed the parcel through the bars.

Recently The Heathen was more subdued, hopeless even. It was apparent to The Man that he had been beaten down in some way. He had even started to feel bad for the poor prisoner. As He passed the food to the man behind the bars, He couldn't help but notice the man sitting there in the corner, for what felt like the first time.

The Man had been too afraid to look at The Heathen for some reason He could not explain, but once He'd gotten a good look at him, He saw that The Heathen and he were not so very different. The Heathen there, before Him, did not look like Heathens He had learned about in school. His clothes were not mangled, dirty rags. They were different than His, to be sure, but you could tell, just by looking at them, that much care had gone in to making the garments (even if The Man thought the individual leg portions on the bottom half of The Heathen's attire to be a bit odd).

The Heathen also did not seem very dirty. There was a slight layer of filth and grime covering him, but The Man recalled that He had not seen it there on the day that He first began His employment. It must have gathered over the weeks The Heathen had been held in The Unholy Complex. Also, The Man noted that The Heathen's hair was cropped short. To The Man, that fact alone showed dexterity and even mastery of modern tools, a trait He had been told Heathens lacked. The things that The Man had been taught and the things He was seeing just weren't harmonizing at all.

So The Man stood there, examining The Heathen before Him, and contemplated the implications of him existing the way that he was, in a non-savage form. He did not know how long He stood there staring at The Heathen but when He finally turned around, back to His cart, He was caught by surprise by a Guardian of The Unholy.

As The Man then found out, His presence had been

requested by the overseer of The Complex of Judas: The Watcher of Lost Souls himself.

The Woman had not slept well the night before, and thus, She was exhausted for most of the day. She had just lain in bed, next to Her Partner all night. She had stared at the ceiling above Them and listened to the soft breathing of Their Child.

Long ago, it used to be on nights She couldn't find slumber, when worry or excitement would push sleep further and further away from Her, that She would Pray. She had seen no need in doing that, though, for She knew it would go unanswered and would just wind up to be a waste of wishful thinking. Instead, She had hoped. She had lain there and ticked off all the optimistic possible outcomes and threw out all the pessimistic ones, choosing to think of where She wanted to be and how She would get there, rather than wallow in the pity for things She had not yet lost.

Eventually She was able to doze, but not for very long before She was awoken by the sound of The Child's hunger. It was then She rose from bed and went about Her daily duties, as best as She could. A fog of tiredness remained around Her, though. The night had truly taken a toll.

She found Herself to be short tempered towards Their Child, and even caught Herself thinking that Their Child's representations of The Sun and The Moon today looked just like scribbles on a piece of parchment. When She caught Herself with that thought, She took a moment to quiet Her mind and get Her thoughts in order. She knew She was being irrational. She knelt down to The Little One and apologized for being in bad spirits throughout the day. After She said Her peace, She brought out a utensil of Her own and began to draw with Their Child on the same parchment.

It's then that The Man burst in.

He entered in a state of utter consternation, and it took Him awhile to put His thoughts into words. What He eventually told Her was enough to make Her feel as if all the blood had rushed from Her face and neck. She felt like She might faint as He told Her of His meeting with The Watcher of Lost Souls.

He explained that, as He feared, His exchange (if it could even be called that) with The Whore had been heard and seen by The Watcher himself. The

Watcher told Him that it was a great cause for concern. The Watcher had said that he had been doing his job for years and felt that perhaps there was some merit in accusations thrown out by the wicked. They usually had a knack for smelling out like-minded individuals. The Man was then quickly reassured that He shouldn't have any immediate concerns, that He seemed like a perfect, upstanding Citizen and a valuable member of The City. The Watcher and the rest of The Pious Commonwealth, He was told, just wanted to make sure The Whore was not on to something.

Immediately after He had finished telling Her all about it, He grabbed some parchment and the utensil from the table by Their Child and then headed into the bathroom, quickly. At first She listened at the door, for fear that a flogging was in order, but all She could hear was the scratching of utensil on parchment.

She then decided to just sit back in Her chair and try to wrap Her mind around what She'd been told as He took His time writing whatever He needed to write. As She sat there, absentmindedly watching Their Child play with Its blocks, She fidgeted with whatever She could get Her fingers on. If The Pious

Commonwealth were to keep a close eye on Her and Her Partner, the truth of Them would most definitely be seen. She knew They could hide Their true feelings from The Pious Commonwealth, but They would not be able to do so forever.

As She helped The Child pick up Its blocks and ready It for bed, The Man exited the bathroom and showed Her what He'd been writing. It was a letter. She sat there and read it, and by the end of it She found that She was sobbing. She then looked up to The Man, seeing the stern look on His face as He reached down to hold Their Child in His arms. She stared at Them both for quite some time before She came to terms with the fact that the letter He wrote must be delivered as soon as possible.

V.

The Man was shaving. He was doing it not because it was mandatory, but rather because He had made the choice to do so. That day was a special day to Him. He contemplated what He was about to do as He brought the razor over His face, washing it off in the sink after each stroke. As He looked at Himself in the mirror He noticed how much He had changed since Pairing Day all those years ago. His eyes were no longer bloodshot, nor were they housed in sunken sockets. They were white and His face fuller. He could tell by the lines around His mouth that He smiled more. He was pleased with His appearance and the changes that had shaped it.

Physical changes were not the only alterations made to The Man. He had also experienced a change in His mind and in His spirits. His thoughts were clearer than they'd ever been and each one had a purpose. He found He was prone to look on the brighter side of things now. His pessimism had all but dissipated. To Him, the world was full of opportunities and He was going to take advantage of as many as He could. In fact, that's the only reason He did not ask for a Redrafting after the incident with The Whore.

Once His face was clear of stubble, He left the compartment after a goodbye from Their Child and a long embrace from His Partner. She then wished Him luck as He walked out of the door and down the corridor towards The Unholy Complex.

As He walked, with vigor in His step, He thought about the plan He had conceived. It started on that day when He had met with The Watcher of Lost Souls. As soon as He walked out of His office, He knew what He must do. He went immediately home and composed a letter. It was a letter rich with entreatment and when He showed it to His Partner, She agreed with the writing of it. He knew He must deliver it as soon as He could.

The following day, He went to His place of employment and made His usually rounds. On that day, however, He lingered outside The Heathen's cell just long enough to tap inconspicuously on the food parcel He was handing in. The Man then walked out of the area, moving quickly, yet without suspicion.

He hoped The Heathen would read the letter He tucked inside the parcel.

On His next visit to The Heathen's cell, He was pleased to have a scrap of paper slipped to Him as He passed the parcel through the bars. It took all the patience He possessed to not read it right then and there. His fortitude prevailed, however, and He was able to get through the rest of His route.

He and His Partner were ecstatic when They finally read The Heathen's response together. Not only did They discover that a lot of Their assumptions about The Pious Commonwealth had been true, in that they were keeping secrets from The Citizens about the state of the world outside, but They also found out that The Heathen was willing to help Them with Their plight. There was just one stipulation: The Man must help The Heathen escape.

A plan needed to be formed.

After a few days of correspondence between the captive and The Man, a concrete solution had been reached and The Man set about collecting the things that The Heathen would require for his act of absconding. They were just odds and ends; things found here and there, small things that could easily be slipped into parcels of food undetected.

After He had delivered the last of the goods, He finished the rest of His route and returned home to His Partner and Child. They had a wonderful supper together, full of hopeful conversation (in hushed tones, of course), and then They settled down for the night. The Man could hardly sleep; He was far too excited. Perhaps it was the lack of sleep that made shaving seem like a good idea.

Now, as He rubbed His clean-shaven face, growing re-accustomed to the boyish feel of it, He walked into The Unholy Complex, His cart with the food parcels being pushed along by His stride. He was half way through His route when He heard someone call out for Him and when He turned He saw The Head Guardian of The Unholy walking towards Him. The Head Guardian had the gravest of news.

It would seem, that somehow, The Heathen, who was a very dangerous man indeed, had escaped sometime during the night. The Man feigned shock and abhorrence. He even acted slightly afraid, glancing around like perhaps The Heathen was hiding in plain sight around them. Of course, it was all façade, for

He Himself had set the event in motion. Yet despite how convincing He felt, He still thought that The Head Guardian looked at Him with distrust and a certain amount of suspicion.

The Man did not fret, though, for He knew in His heart of hearts that He had executed His part of the plan perfectly. All that remained for Him to do was to finish His rounds, calmly but quickly, so that He could begin work on the second part of the plan: freeing The Child from the walls of The City.

The Woman's emotions toward the plan were mixed. When She first heard it, She was sorrowful and didn't understand why She could not go with Her Child. Then, when it was fully explained to Her in detail by Her Partner, She understood. They couldn't risk Their Child losing Its freedom. If They all attempted escape, They would surely be caught, but if it was just The Little One, the risks were lessened. In addition, Her and Her Partner might be forced to take diversionary measures for The Little One to escape unharmed, should the need arise. There was hope, however, for The Man believed that They may be given an opportunity to escape Themselves one day. That is what She hoped for the most.

She had begun to work on Her part of the plan long ago. She had been informed, through The Man through The Heathen, that there was a small passageway out of The City. In the letter The Heathen wrote, the passage had been described as a 'drainage pipe', whatever that meant, and it was not much bigger than Their Child Itself. The 'pipe' would expel water from The River of Eden, out into The Land of The Heathens, and so that is the way Their Child would have to exit The City.

She was reminded of Moses when She heard of what They must do and so She began to work on a basket for The Little One. She used bits and pieces of things She had found around Their compartment. She even ripped them out of the little houses and palaces She and Their Child had built together. Once it was all crafted together in a sturdy fashion, She tested the craft in the washbasin. Upon finding it satisfactory, She began to line it with blankets and pack it with some of the toys that The Little One held dear, including the utensil It had drawn beautiful things with.

Then She laid a tunic of Hers, and one of Her Partner's, at the bottom of the basket, for She so adored the scent of The Child and thought that maybe The Little One would appreciate Their scent as well. Perhaps, in the years to come, the scent might provide fond memories of Them. The Woman knew Their Child was young, and may forget Her anyway, but still She wrapped the tunics tight and placed them in there for It.

There were other little things She wanted The Child to have, and She set about packing them in too. As She went about that task Her Partner returned home. She could tell by the look on His face and the way He approached Her that He felt the same way about the departure as She did. All They could do was embrace.

As His Partner finished packing the basket, The Man stared at Their Child with sadness in His eyes. He contemplated saying goodbye. It seemed like it had not been that long since The Little One came into Their lives, yet, at the same time, it felt like it could have happened forever ago. Their Child had become a staple of Their existence, a unique and precious thing, that helped Them grow and solidified Their already strong beliefs against The Pious Commonwealth. Without The Little One, He could not fathom where He would be. He found that He did not know where to begin in the ordeal that would be His last farewell to Their Child.

Instead, He just knelt down beside It and began to play. He playfully attacked The Little One, who squealed with delight and ran about the compartment. He made strange noises as He chased Their giggling Child around. Its giggles made Him chuckle and once He caught It; They collapsed on the floor, in a heap of joy, and laughed until They were out of breath. He then hoisted It up, above Him and They, Their Child and He, looked at one another. Their laughter stopped but Their smiles stayed. As He looked into Their Child's eyes, He saw the entirety of Their past together and His heart nearly broke right then.

They continued to play for hours after that, but it felt like no time had passed at all. When His Partner walked in. She said She was done with Her task of packing the basket and that supper was almost ready for Them.

As They all ate, The Woman sung Them a song She had composed Herself. It was beautiful and the magic and whimsy in Their Child's eyes as It watched Its Mother sing, almost made it too much for The Man to bear. He endured, with much difficultly, and made it through supper without a single tear being shed.

After the table had been cleared and the extra food was put away, The Man sat down and read The Little One a story The Woman had written. It was a wonderful story about wonderful things, but The Child was too tired to truly be captivated. The Little One's eyes began to close. At first, it was slow blinks; once the eyes had shut, they would shoot open again. It was an adorable gesture that The Man took to mean that Their Child wanted to spend as much time with Them as possible. Soon, however, the eyes closed and stayed closed, and the soft breath of slumber could be heard.

The Man put the story away, back in the closet, and then He stood there holding Their Child in His arms. Before He called His Partner over to put It to bed, He took a few moments to really feel The Little One in His arms. He rocked It softly and squeezed It gently, staring at Its peaceful face as It slept. He then began to whisper to It.

The Man knew The Little One could not hear Him, yet He felt compelled to tell The Child that He cared for It deeply and that He only wanted what is best for It. He said that if there were any other way to accomplish Their task, He would do it in a heartbeat. He would keep Their Child forever if He could. As He continued to whisper, It slept on moving about slightly. He didn't want to wake It, for It needed Its sleep for the journey ahead, but He needed It to know. He told Their Child of the great things It would now be able to accomplish if It wanted to. It would now be free. The Man explained that He was giving The Child freedom. A freedom He Himself had never had and, because He had never had it, He knew He owed it to The Little One. It was a strange feeling, and He had trouble putting it into words for Their Child, but He tried His best to reiterate that in order to give It all the possibilities the world held, It needed to be free from the walls of The City. He then whispered three more sweet words into Their Child's ear before He called over His Partner.

Once She had taken The Little One from His hands and went to carry It off to Its crib, The Man felt as though He might weep. Instead, He went to the bathroom and started running the shower. He thought that bathing could, maybe, calm His racing mind.

As She carried The Little One to Its crib, She quietly

sang It one last song. She gazed upon It as She walked. She could not believe that when She had first laid eyes upon It, Their beautiful Child, that She had thought of It as nothing more than a chore or a burden. Yet now as She laid It down in the crib for the last time, She wondered what She would do now that It was going to be out of Her life.

Who would She draw with? Who would enjoy Her stories? Who would She sing to? She knew that She still had Her Partner, but He was a muse of a different kind for different stories and different songs. She didn't like the thought of never drawing for Her Child again.

Once She placed It into the crib, She felt the urge to pick It right back up again. She knew that would not be wise, for Their Child needed sleep for Its travels. So She just watched It sleep. She found Herself wishing that The Child were older. How badly She wanted to ask It what It would think of the whole ordeal that was to transpire on Its behalf. She liked to think that The Little One (were It not so little) would want to stay with Her. That might cause more problems, however, and so She settled on being as glad as She could be that the decision was purely Hers and Her Partner's to make.

It then dawned on Her that The Man had been in the shower for quite some time. She decided, with much internal debate, to leave Their sleeping Child and check on The Man to make sure He wasn't overly concerned about the task at hand. So She pressed Her lips on to The Little One's forehead and walked out of the room as quietly as possible.

She found The Man crouched in the shower, just letting the water wash over Him. It was slightly concerning to see Him so vulnerable, but He was wont to do that and She pushed Her worry aside. She decided to disrobe and join Him there, under the water. He did not seem to notice She had entered until She placed Her hand on His back and Her lips upon His shoulder. She smiled a feeble smile as He turned to Her, and returned the expression. There was sorrow in His eyes, despite the smile on His face. She then pulled His face to Hers and touched Her lips to His. He grabbed Her face in return and pulled Her closer in a display of passion. Soon, They were embraced, Their arms wrapped around each other's nude bodies, lips-upon-lips and chest-upon-chest. Just when She thought He would enter Her, He stopped and put His arms on Her shoulders.

His eyes were ripe with a different sort of passion as

He explained to Her that He would rather just talk with Her, like They used to. Despite Her initial insecurities, She indulged Him and They sat there, on the wet floor of the shower, and discussed everything They could. He showered Her with adorations and told Her of the great things that both They and Their Child would accomplish as She regaled Him with Her concerns about The Little One's forthcoming journey and Her hopes for The Little One. She confessed that She wished Their Little One would remember the plight of Its parents and raise a rebellion from outside The City's walls. They then conversed about what could be out there, in The Land of The Heathens. They both expressed worry as to whether or not it would be satisfactory enough for Their Child. They went on and on like that for quite awhile. Then The Sunset Bell rang.

As soon as He heard the tone of The Sunset Bell, He told His Partner that They should ready Themselves. Quickly, They dried off and dawned the darkest tunics They owned. The Woman put Her hair up, and then the two of Them entered the bedroom as quietly as They could.

She went to The Child in Its crib and began to pick It

up as Her Partner grabbed the basket She had made and went to the door. He opened it a crack and peeked out in the corridor. He was positive that He would see A Guardian standing there, for He was under watch after all, yet when He opened the door fully and looked up and down the corridor, He saw that no one was in the dimly lit passageway.

The Man turned to His Partner, Their Child in Her arms, and motioned for Her to wait in the compartment for a moment. Then, He placed the basket on the ground and walked out into the corridor. He looked for anyone who could be watching for Them. After He'd walked around a bit, and turned many corners with much covertness, He began to think Himself a fool.

Suddenly, it dawned on Him what a truly terrible place The City was. It was nothing more than a palace built of fear and lies. All of it; The Watcher's suspicion, the vow to have Him and His Family watched, even the threat of constant Guardians had all been used to try and control Him, and like a fool, He had fallen for it. Yet, the joke was on them, for He prepared for the worst, but the worst never planned on coming. He was, at the moment, glad His Child had the ability to escape The City. It was a place that tried to take anything and everything it could from anybody who resided here. It would not take anything from The Little One, though. That The Man was sure of. He had never been more positive of anything in His entire life.

He then walked back to the compartment, habitually looking over His shoulder and cursing every time He did so. The Woman and Their Child, who was still fast asleep, were waiting at the door anxiously. The Man grabbed the basket that His Partner had made and, with great confidence, motioned for The Woman to follow Him. He led Their Child and Her down the corridor towards The River of Eden and The Little One's freedom.

They moved silently, in quick bursts through the crossways. As She held The Child, still fast asleep, The Man held the basket and kept a stern eye on Their surroundings. Every now and then They would stop, so that He could peer around a corner or investigate a shadow, just to be safe. Some moments She could have sworn She heard something, but Her Partner comforted Her. He doubted that anyone would be after Them; the noises She thought She heard were merely the effects of the fear The Pious

Commonwealth had instilled in Her. She realized that to be true, and carried on, following Her Partner and ignoring the bumps and muffled whispers that were nothing more than figments spawned by paranoia.

Before too much longer, They entered The Grand Hall of Gathering. They could see through the darkness The River of Eden flowing. She recalled how She once thought The Grand Hall was beautiful. It could have been the current lighting or, more likely, Her current mindset, but She no longer saw the splendor She once had seen.

In one of the letters The Heathen wrote, he talked about natural rivers; water running through grass or dirt or sand under the vacant sky, not on stone through walls and ceilings. She yearned to see that kind of natural construction and not the man-made, water-on-stone monstrosity. She was so glad She could give that gift to Their Child.

She was thankful for the sorry excuse for a river now: it would be The Little One's passage out of the manufactured place. Their Child would get to see the world as it was meant to. It would get to gaze upon The Sun and The Moon. She found Herself wondering if Their Child would think of Her when It saw them.

The Man called to Her in a hushed whisper and that brought Her back from Her mind. She looked over to Him and He waved for Her to come to the Statue of St. Peter that He was crouching behind. He then rubbed His eyes in an attempt to get them used to the darkness. Once He'd seen that They were all alone there, He guided Her and Their Child to The River's edge.

Once there, She looked at Their Child in Her arms and thought for a second about turning back; it wasn't too late. She shook the thought away, reminding Herself of the greater good for The Little One, and watched as The Man put the basket into the water. He then turned to Her and They made eye contact. She nodded softly, a gesture He returned, and then placed Their Child into Its basket, covering It tightly with Their tunics. She then placed Her lips on Its forehead and held them there, never wanting that moment to end. She whispered goodbye to It and then watched as The Man loosened His grip on the basket, letting the water take Their Child to some place better.

She wept then. Not in sorrow or in pain, but in the

hope that She felt. Hope that The Little One would remember Her as more than a Rearer or caregiver. Hope that She was a presence in Its life that shaped what It would become.

The Man watched Their Child drift off to freedom as He held His Partner in His arms. As He watched The Little One go, there in the silence of The Grand Hall of Gathering, He realized fully what He had done:

He had achieved the impossible.

He and His Partner had breathed new life into Their Child, who was now floating down The River. The life that had been breathed would be a life full of promise, not the bleak, hopeless life He, like so many others in The City, had been taught was the pinnacle of existence. He'd achieved that all by purely realizing that He could and with that realization He breathed a new life into His Partner and Himself.

He knew, with all certainty, that there would be no repercussions for His actions as long as He could keep what He had done to Himself. He would blame Their missing Child on the escaped Heathen and would be showered with pity. A pity He could then use as a veil to plot and plan further against The Pious Commonwealth. It was a truly exciting revelation.

He smiled with tears in His eyes and looked down at His Partner as She watched the basket travel through the archway and into the darkness. They stood there for some time, watching after The Little One in Its basket, listening closely to anything and everything that would tell Them if Their Child was okay or not. It was silent.

As He walked His Partner back to Their compartment, He knew it would be hard to readjust without Their Child in Their home, but He had Faith in Their Child and the things It would achieve. It wasn't the same kind of Faith that He had been raised to have. Not a Faith in some Being who pulls the cords of life at its whim, but rather a Faith in the world as it worked. For now, because of The Child, He saw the spark in everything and it lit a flame that yearns for life. The City liked to extinguish that flame, to blind The Citizens from the spark, so that true Faith could not grow inside of them. Yet, because of what He and His Partner had just done Their Child's spark could ignite and it would not be extinguished once It was outside the walls of The

City. He had absolute Faith in that. It was because of that Faith that He knew, deep down inside of Himself, that They would see Their Child again.

Acknowledgements:
Without my mother I wouldn't be here,
Without my father I wouldn't create,
Without my family I would have nothing,
And without Leah I would be no one.
Thank you.

About the Author

Nicolas Ryan Moore is a writer, filmmaker, and artist who currently resides in The Pacific Northwest. This is his first published book and he hopes that you have liked it.

If you'd like more information or if you would like to help him on his journey, please visit his Patreon page at **www.patreon.com/nrm**.

This has been a publication from:

Idea Machine Output.

Idea Machine Output is a collective of writers and artists based in The Pacific Northwest. They produce books, films, and other materials.

For more information visit their website:

IdeaMachineOutput.com

or email them at info@ideamachineoutput.com

www.ingramcontent.com/pod-product-compliance
Lightning Source LLC
Chambersburg PA
CBHW061253170626
46809CB00007B/2975

* 9 7 8 0 6 9 2 8 6 9 1 0 9 *